Produced by Kroha Associates, Inc.
Middletown, Connecticut

Illustrated by Yakovetic Productions

Written by M.C. Varley

Printed in the United States of America.

ISBN 1-56326-168-5

How Does Your Garden Grow?

One day, while the little fish Sandy was out exploring, she came across a beautiful garden in a part of the ocean where she had never been before. It was a wonderful place, full of lush green vines and brightly colored flowers.

What a great place to play hide-and-seek, Sandy thought to herself, as she went to get her brother Flounder. Soon they were both frolicking in the garden.

"Close your eyes," Sandy shouted. "Count to three, and then see if you can find me!"

Flounder shut his eyes tight. "One, two, three!" he called. "Ready or not, here I come!" Then Flounder looked around and began to search for his sister. But even though he peeked behind the flowering sea poppy vines and between the acadia blossoms, he couldn't find Sandy anywhere. "You can come out now!" he shouted. "I give up!"

"Boo!" Sandy cried, darting out of the vines right in front of Flounder. "I got you!"

"You sure did!" agreed Flounder. "This is a great place to play! Let's go get Ariel! She'll love it here!"

Hidden behind a tangle of vines, the eels Flotsam and Jetsam watched Flounder and Sandy playing. The eels belonged to the evil sea witch, Ursula, and they didn't like seeing the little fish having so much fun.

"Perhaps if we destroyed the garden," Jetsam suggested, "Flounder and Sandy wouldn't be quite so happy all the time."

"Yes," Flotsam hissed back. "Spoiling their silly game sounds splendid! Let's eat that scrumptious garden up."

And so, as soon as Flounder and Sandy were out of sight, Flotsam and Jetsam began to eat the beautiful garden.

Meanwhile, Flounder and Sandy were telling the Little Mermaid all about the special spot Sandy had found. "It's the most fantastic place under the sea!" Flounder exclaimed.

"We can't wait for you to see it, Ariel," Sandy told her. "Come and play hide-and-seek with us right now!"

"I'd love to," Ariel replied. "But it's too late to play anymore today. We'll have to wait until tomorrow."

All the while the eels continued to eat. "Not only will this spoil their fun," Flotsam said between mouthfuls, "but these orange flowers are particularly tasty, too!"

"Except for all the pesky seeds!" Jetsam said, spitting a mouthful of the shiny, black kernels onto the ocean floor. "Make sure you eat everything else, though. We don't want a single hiding place left!"

The next morning, when Sandy led Ariel and Flounder back to where the garden had been, everything was changed. The vines lay in tatters, and all that was left of the beautiful flowers were one or two half-eaten petals and a sprinkling of seeds.

"Are you sure this is the right place?" asked Ariel.

"This *was* the place," Sandy replied. "Who could have done such a terrible thing?"

Just then they heard a groaning sound coming from behind a rock. It was Flotsam and Jetsam! "Ooooh," they complained, their bellies bulging from all the vines and flowers they had eaten. "We feel awful!"

Sandy was heartbroken. "I can't believe even Ursula's eels would do such a thing," she said sadly.

"Let's go tell Sebastian," Ariel suggested. "Maybe he'll know what to do."

And so Ariel, Flounder, and Sandy swam to the island as fast as they could. "I hope the garden can be saved," Sebastian told them. "But it doesn't sound as if there is much left. Let's go back and take a look."

On their journey back under the sea, Sebastian told his friends the story of a human town where the people had wanted wood to build their buildings. They cut down all the trees for lumber, but they didn't think about what would happen next. Without the trees, the sun dried up all the land until it turned into a desert.

"No trees! How horrible!" Sandy cried. "What did they do?"

"Exactly what we're going to do," Sebastian told her as they arrived at what had once been the garden. He picked up a handful of the precious seeds the eels had spit out. "The humans planted seeds and hoped that new plants would grow to replace the old ones."

Everyone joined in planting the new garden. Ariel and Sebastian dug the holes, making sure they weren't too deep. Then Sandy dropped the seeds in one at a time, and Flounder covered them with sand with a quick flip of his tail.

But when they were finished, Sandy started to cry. "It didn't work!" she sobbed. "The seeds aren't growing! There must be something wrong with them!"

"No, there isn't, Sandy," the Little Mermaid told her. "It just takes time for seeds to grow—a lot longer than it took for the eels to destroy the garden."

Sandy was sad that her favorite place wouldn't grow back overnight. Still, she was determined to take care of it until every seed had sprouted and grown new flowers.

Every day Sandy went to the garden and tended to the rows of seeds they had planted. She made sure that no weeds grew there, and kept a lookout in case the eels should return.

It was hard work, and sometimes Sandy wondered whether it was worth it. But then one day a tiny vine burst forth from the ocean floor. The garden was growing! Sandy was thrilled — especially when she saw, at the very tip of the fragile new vine, a little bud getting ready to blossom!

Soon the entire garden was in bloom again.

"Congratulations, Sandy! You did a great job," Ariel told her friend.

"We all helped, but nature helped the most," Sandy said. "It's sad to think the garden could have disappeared forever."

"But it didn't, Sandy!" Flounder said happily. "Now we can play hide-and-seek again. Close your eyes, count to three, and then find Ariel and me!"